THE PRICKLY PORCUPINE

by Dawn Bentley
Illustrated by Beth Stover

For Nile Alexander Bentley—

"Why didn't the skeleton cross the road? 'Cause he didn't have any guts!"

You always make me laugh! I love you so much! — D.B.

Published by Soundprints Division of Trudy Corporation, Norwalk, Connecticut.

Book design: Marcin D. Pilchowski
Editor: Laura Gates Galvin
Editorial assistance: Chelsea Shriver

First Edition 2003
10 9 8 7 6 5 4 3 2 1
Printed in China

3-24-06

Acknowledgments:
  Our very special thanks to Dr. Don E. Wilson of the Department of Systematic Biology at the Smithsonian Institution's National Museum of Natural History for his curatorial review.
  Soundprints would also like to thank Ellen Nanney and Robyn Bissette at the Smithsonian Institution's Office of Product Development and Licensing for their help in the creation of this book.
  Many thanks to Laura Gates Galvin, my editor-extraordinaire, who made this project a joy to work on! (D.B.)

Library of Congress Cataloging-in-Publication Data

Bentley, Dawn.
    The prickly porcupine / by Dawn Bentley ; illustrated by Beth Stover.
        p. cm.
    Summary: Porcupine defends herself, and, later, her baby, from their enemy, the fisher, by using the hard, sharp quills that cover her body.
    ISBN 1-59249-013-1 (pbk.)
    1. Porcupines—Juvenile fiction. [1. Porcupines—Fiction.] I. Stover, Beth, 1969- ill.
    II. Title.

PZ10.3.B4517 Pr 2003
[E]—dc21

                                                                2002191154

Table of Contents

Chapter 1: It's Porcupine!   5

Chapter 2: Come Down, Porcupine   15

Chapter 3: Porcupine's Sharp Quills   25

Chapter 4: Porcupine Has a Baby   35

Glossary   44

Wilderness Facts about the Porcupine   45

A note to the reader:
Throughout this story you will see words in **bold letters**.
There is more information about these words in the
glossary. The glossary is in the back of the book.

Chapter 1

It's Porcupine!

High in a tree,
something moves.
It looks like a bird's
nest. It is not a nest.
It is a porcupine!

Porcupine has long hairs. Her hairs make her look like a nest. Sometimes her enemies think she *is* a nest.

The hairs on Porcupine are called **quills**. The quills are hard and very sharp.

Porcupine eats in the trees. Porcupine sleeps in the trees. In winter, Porcupine stays in the trees for weeks!

Some animals are busy in the day. Porcupine sleeps in the day. Porcupine is busy at night.

Chapter 2

Come Down, Porcupine

The sun is down.

The moon is out.

Porcupine is ready to explore the forest.

Porcupine looks
for things to eat.
She does not hurry.
She has all night!

A **beaver** chews on a tree. Porcupine cannot see the beaver. Porcupine can only see things that are very close.

Water lilies

float in a pond.

Porcupine eats

one. She enjoys

her snack.

Chapter 3

Porcupine's Sharp Quills

Porcupine loves to eat twigs. She loves to eat bark, too. Bark is one of the foods she likes best!

Porcupine hears something. Porcupine smells something. It is a **fisher**. The fisher is her enemy!

The fisher is not
scared of Porcupine.
Porcupine raises
her quills. Porcupine
chatters her teeth.
Porcupine stomps
her feet.

Porcupine turns around. She lifts her tail. She shows the fisher her sharp quills.

Porcupine swings her
tail. Her tail hits the
fisher in the face.
Ouch! The fisher
runs away.

Chapter 4

Porcupine
Has a Baby

Today, Porcupine
is going to have a
baby! She does not
go back to her tree.

In a hollow log,
Porcupine has one
tiny baby. He can
walk soon after
he is born!

One day later,
Baby leaves the
log. Porcupine
climbs up a tree.
She wants Baby
to follow.

Porcupine chatters to Baby. Baby follows slowly. Baby learns quickly! Porcupine will teach Baby many more things.

Soon, Baby will live on his own. For now, Porcupine will protect Baby as they rest high in the tree.

Glossary

Beaver: a rodent that lives both in water and on land. Beavers have webbed hind feet and broad, flat tails.

Fisher: a weasel found in North America.

Quills: needle-like spines that cover most of a porcupine's body.

Water lily: a plant that grows in the water, with floating leaves and big flowers.

Wilderness Facts About the Porcupine

Porcupines have about 30,000 sharp hairs called quills. Quills are about 2 to 3 inches long. Each quill has tiny spikes that make it hard to remove from the skin. When a porcupine loses a quill, it grows back. It takes two to eight months for a quill to grow.

Porcupines are rodents, like rats, beavers and squirrels. A rodent is a mammal whose front teeth never stop growing. Porcupines keep their front teeth the right length by chewing on tree bark.

Full-grown porcupines are about 3 feet long. They weigh between 11 and 13 pounds—that is the size of a house cat.

Animals that live near porcupines in the Atlantic wilderness include:

Beavers

Black bears

Eastern chipmunks

Eastern gray squirrels

Fishers

Little brown bats

Moose

Raccoons

Red foxes

Striped skunks

White-tailed deer

Wood frogs